The text of this book is set in Comic Sans MS, Minion and Spumoni
The illustrations are rendered in ink on paper

Printed in China

Bob Winging it / written by Yousef (Joe) Jamaldinian & Meredith Self.
          illustrated by Yousef (Joe) Jamaldinian.

Summary: A penguin named Bob dreams of traveling to warm places and learns to fly to escape the cold weather.
ISBN 0-9766657-0-0

Bob
Winging It

By Joe Jamaldinian and Meredith Self

This is Bob.
There is only one thing Bob doesn't like.

Bob really, really doesn't like to be cold.
That's odd for a penguin, he was always told.

Bob tried everything to keep from feeling the cold shivering weather. Drinking hot cocoa always made Bob feel better.

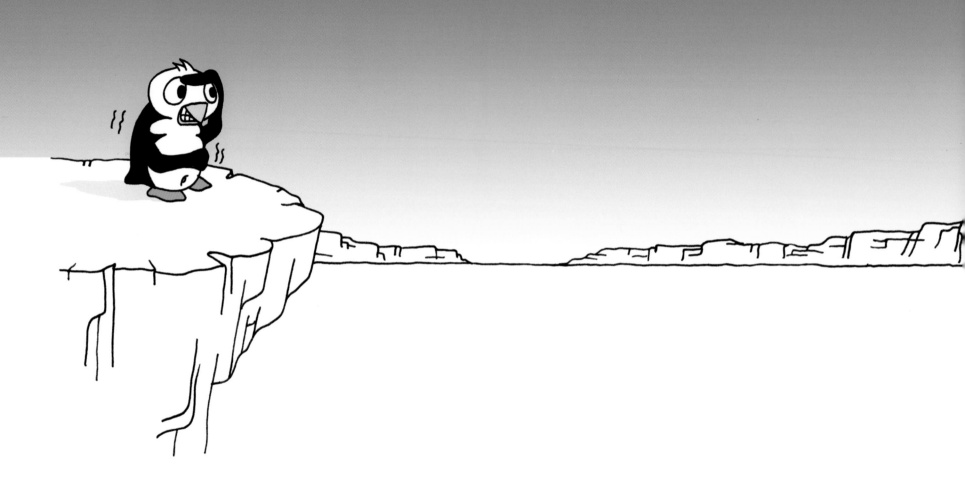

Every day Bob waddled to the highest ice peak,
but he never saw a warm place within his reach.
Bob wanted to see something other than ice—
some place with palm trees would be quite nice.

One day Bob looked up at the puffins in the sky
and thought how great it would be if he could fly.
He wondered about all the warm places he would see
and how fun and exciting it would be.

But not everyone thought Bob's wondering was wonderful.

"You can't fly with those silly little wings.
You're always dreaming up crazy things!"

Those teasing penguins made Bob sad
and feeling so cold was making him mad.
"Don't give up, Bob," his Momma said.
"Get some advice from wise Grandpa instead."

"That's a great idea! A penguin in the sky!
Your heart says fly," Grandpa said. "Why not try?"

So Bob did.

Crash!!

"Maybe I've been going about this wrong.
I've been using contraptions all along.
I can use my wings and heart, not just my head.
Isn't that what Grandpa said?"

The puffins were surprised by what Bob asked
but they agreed to help with this unusual task.

He'd have to get his wings strong first.
Working out so hard made Bob's feathers hurt.

But he wouldn't give up.

Just one more push up...

Then the puffins showed Bob how they flew.
Bob wasn't sure if he could do it too.

His wings and muscles finally grew big and strong.
He imagined super hero strength that couldn't go wrong.

It was time for Bob to try again.

Bob thought positive thoughts
then ran and ran and...

Whooosh... Woooooooo... Bob finally flew!

"I'm flying! I'm flying!"
Bob screamed from the skies.
The other penguins couldn't believe their eyes.

Bob couldn't stop smiling! He wouldn't stop flying!
He was thrilled that he never quit and kept on trying.

With joy Bob flew
all around the world.

He saw friendly new faces
and great warm places.

Bob was glad he followed his heart and used his head.
Instead of ice Bob enjoyed his warm comfy tree bed.